To:

From:

How to Catch a Gingerbread Man

From the *New York Times*
Bestselling Team
Adam Wallace &
Andy Elkerton

sourcebooks
wonderland

Once upon a **story time** at the bookstore down the street, some friends come in to have some fun— they're in for quite a treat!

Story time TODAY!

Sitting at the story rug
with a special book in hand,
the reading is about to begin
about me, the Gingerbread Man...

"Run, run, as fast as you can,"
the storyteller starts to read.

So out I pop, right off the page
and break away with **speed**!

You kids will never catch me–
I'm much too fast for you!

Especially when I have help
from the *boy who never grew*!

This clever trap won't do the trick–
you need a **magic spell**!
And with a wizard on my side,
your traps won't do so well.

You don't need COURAGE, BRAINS, OR HEART—
you've got plenty of those!
You only need a better trap
to keep me on my toes!

You thought this trap would really fool
the WORLD'S GREATEST DETECTIVE?
He sees right through your wise disguise—

it seems your trap's defective!

Now your traps are getting better,
I admit, I am impressed.

TWANG!

But **Robin Hood** just saved the day.
I think he's just the best!

The Merry Adventures of Robin Hood

A bow tie, buttons, even pants!?

This place has everything!

But something here is not quite right...

what's with this great big spring?

What a big trap you had here!

The better to catch me with, I think.

Too bad my friends helped me escape—

I'm up and gone in a blink!

This trap you set was no big deal.

It's broken now, but how?

Perhaps the boy with **magic beans** saved me with his cow...

Alice and her **mad-hat** friends,

as a gift for my unbirthday,

helped guide me through the walls of shelves—

now I'm *bound* to find my way.

What a great day! I'm having fun—
you youngsters sure are bright!
But have you given up on me?
There's not a TRAP in sight...

I've won again! And I must say,
this trap wasn't half-bad.
But as I take my **victory lap**,
I notice you look sad...

I may be free, but now I want
to see your smiles and laughter!
So back I go to give this tale
a **happily ever after...**

Run, run as fast as you can.

Can *you* catch me?

I'm the Gingerbread Man!

Published by Sourcebooks Wonderland, an imprint of Sourcebooks Kids
P.O. Box 4410, Naperville, Illinois 60567-4410
(630) 961-3900
sourcebookskids.com

Library of Congress Cataloging-in-Publication Data is on file with the publisher.
Source of Production: Wing King Tong Paper Products Co. Ltd., Shenzhen,
Guangdong Province, China
Date of Production: April 2021
Run Number: 5021348

Printed and bound in China.

WKT 10 9 8 7 6 5 4 3 2 1